MIRROR, MIRROR

Writer: Jason Hernandez Rosenblatt
Illustrators: Joe Staton and Dan Davis Colorist: Dan Waters

Dalmatian Press, LLC, 2003. All rights reserved. Printed in the U.S.A.
The DALMATIAN PRESS name and logo are trademarks of Dalmatian Press, LLC, Franklin, Tennessee 37067.
No part of this book may be reproduced or copied in any form without written permission from the copyright owner.

05 06 07 08 LBM 10 9 8 7 6 5 4

12548 JUSTICE LEAGUE: Mirror, Mirror

Central City was under attack! From their Watchtower headquarters in orbit above Earth, the mighty Justice League heard the call for help.

"Wonder who's making trouble this time," mused the Flash as he raced ahead of his teammates.

"As fast as you run," responded Green Lantern, "you'll be the first to find out... as usual!"

Faster than the eye can see, the fired-up Flash super-sped to the scene of the crime. But as he turned the corner onto busy Broome Street, he stopped short — and his blood ran cold.

"Uh-oh," said the Scarlet Speedster. "Everything's covered in ice! And that's usually a crystal-clear sign that one frosty super-villain is back in town!"

From sidewalks to rooftops, Broome Street was coated in thick ice. And that was the calling card of a certain small-time crook who, with the long-ago theft of the plans to an amazing freeze-gun, had more than once put the freeze on Central City — and earned himself a place as one of the Flash's most dangerous foes!

"Captain Cold!" exclaimed the Scarlet Speedster.

"The one and only," laughed the villain. "And I'm here to put this whole city on ice... including the police!"

Captain Cold aimed his treacherous freeze-gun at a police car, instantly sealing it in ice.

The Flash raced toward the car to save the two policemen who were struggling to get out before they froze.

But before the Flash could reach the trapped policemen and use his super-friction to melt the ice, he was suddenly under attack!

"Oww! Ow! Ow!" the Scarlet Speedster cried out.

A barrage of boomerangs was battering him from behind. Once again, the Fastest Man Alive did not need to see this attacking villain to know his name.

"Captain Boomerang!"

From down under in Australia came "Digger" Harkness to make his illegal fortune in America. Using his native weapon with great skill, Captain Boomerang was another of the Flash's regular foes.

"Right you are, mate," laughed the villain. "Like my trusty boomerangs, I always come back!"

The Flash's rogue opponents believed they had the Scarlet Speedster outnumbered, but a pair of deflecting bracelets, a green power ring, searing heat vision, and a well-aimed Batarang quickly proved them wrong.

"These guys giving you any trouble, Flash?" asked Green Lantern.

"These guys?" said Flash with a smile. "They're no trouble at all!"

"Don't be so blinkin' sure, Flash," said Captain Boomerang with a sly grin. "I suggest you mind your yabberin', 'cause I might just surprise you."

"Let's go, Boomerang," shouted Captain Cold.

"No worries, Cold! Hooroo, super zeros!" called Boomerang as the two crooks took off down Broome Street.

Ahead of the villains was the Broome Building, covered from sidewalk to rooftop with a thick, mirror-like coat of ice.

"The doors and windows are frozen over," said Batman. "We've got them cornered."

"Guess again, Batman," said Captain Cold.

But before the Dark Knight Detective could fathom the meaning of the frigid felon's puzzling comment, a brilliant burst of light exploded before the super heroes' eyes.

The mirror-like ice on the building in front of them glowed with the images of the startled super heroes.

"What... what has happened to me?" Hawkgirl fluttered.
"I can hardly stand up!"

"Don't ask me," Batman said. "Everything's so... confusing!"

"Can't think straight," Green Lantern moaned. "Must concentrate... to make my ring work...!"

"That bright light," Superman gasped. "It's done something to us!"

"Indeed it has, Superman," said the voice of the masked face that appeared on the wall. "Thanks to me – Mirror Master!

"Cold and Boomerang did their jobs well! They lured you into my trap where I exposed you to my Mirror Ray, turning all of you into mirror images of yourselves and reversing your strengths into weaknesses."

With a cruel laugh, Mirror Master faded away, saying, "And with the Justice League reduced to helpless weaklings, my friends and I are free to rob this city blind!"

"Batman! Superman! The villains are escaping!" cried a policeman.

But the world's greatest heroes, changed by the Mirror Ray to the world's weakest beings, were mere reflections of their former selves, powerless to help!

The team managed to get to the Watchtower, where they sat in helpless silence as Captain Cold, Captain Boomerang, and Mirror Master stole from the good citizens of Central City.

"I'm so confused," was all Batman could say.

"Great," said Flash angrily. "Batman used to be the brains of this group... just like I was once the fastest man alive. But Mirror Master's trap reversed all our powers, so now all I can do is sit here."

"Just sit here," the Flash grumbled again, slumping over the table. Then, slowly, the Flash sat up straight.

"Sit here…" he repeated, with a bright smile, "…and think! Now that I'm not so busy running all over the place, I've had time to think — and I've actually come up with a plan!"

"Amazing," said Martian Manhunter.

Later that day in Central City, the villainous trio fled the scene of a crime on Captain Cold's ice slide.

"All the loot we can carry... and no heroes to stop us," laughed Captain Cold.

"Good onya for that mirror gimmick, mate," said Boomerang.

"A work of genius," agreed Mirror Master, "if I do say so myself!"

"Not so fast, boys," rang out a familiar voice.

Suddenly, the frozen getaway slide was blocked by the Justice League.
A smirking Flash stood in the front.

"Guess which band of heroes found a way to undo the effects of your
Mirror Ray," he said.

"Can… can they do that?" asked a worried Captain Boomerang.

"Who cares?" snarled Mirror Master. "The Justice League can undo it all they want… and I'll keep re-doing it every time we meet!"

With that, Mirror Master pulled the special Mirror Ray from his belt and took aim at the heroes. "Make me an ice mirror, Captain Cold!"

"Give it your best shot, MM," said the Flash.
"Oh, I will, you fleet-footed fool," said Mirror Master.
"Mirror's ready, pal," said Captain Cold.

Once again, the heroes of the Justice League were
bathed in a bright light reflected off an ice mirror!
And, as the light faded...

...the Justice League exploded into action — coming out from where they had been hiding in a nearby alleyway.

"Well, how do you like that," laughed the Flash as he super-sped through a paper-thin mirrored surface that had been stretched across the street, angled toward the alleyway. "Looks like we fooled Mirror Master — with a mirror!"

"That was the plan," said Green Lantern. "We made them believe we had gotten our powers back by showing ourselves to them in a mirror."

"Yes," said Superman, as he melted Mirror Master's weapon with his heat vision. "So when Mirror Master used his Mirror Ray this time, it reflected off our mirror onto us — and reversed us back to normal."

"Oh, blimey," moaned Captain Boomerang.

As the police took the villains off to jail, Green Lantern patted his teammate on the back.

"That was some fast thinking, Flash," said the Emerald Crusader.

"It sure was," agreed the Scarlet Speedster. "But now that everything's back to normal, I think I'll stick to what I do best."

"That," said Batman, "sounds like the second best idea you've ever had, Flash."